Mom

Donna Todd

White Bird Publications
P.O. Box 90145
Austin, Texas 78709
http://www.whitebirdpublications.com

Copyright©2017 by Donna Todd
Cover by E. Kusch

LCCN: 2017935190
ISBN: 978-1-63363-222-6

PRINTED IN THE UNITED STATES OF AMERICA

Contents

Dedication

In loving memory of my mother, Donnie

Acknowledgements

Writing a book is a solo endeavor but the experience is enriched when you have great people in your life, sharing in your pursuit.

Many thanks to everyone at White Bird publishing: the astute and attentive Evelyn Byrne-Kusch. Your talent and enthusiasm made it possible to publish this book. Also, to Jean and Cat for their meticulous editing skills. You are a fabulous team. Thank you for believing in me.

A huge thank you to those who read early drafts, laughed at Mom's antics and encouraged me to write more of her stories: Sandy Battista, Doug Lyle, Terri Nolan, Craig Strickland, Laurie Thomas, and Barbara Varma. You all make the process of reading and editing so enjoyable, I look forward to every one of our writer's group meetings. I am grateful to Dave Ciambrone, whose early support and friendship kept me writing for all these years.

And a special thank you to my guys, sometimes my first readers but always my greatest supporters: My wonderful husband Steve, whose quick wit makes life fun and keeps laughter in the house. You are always willing to listen and understand my desire to write. That means so much. My sons, Danny and Eric, who have both been gifted with a wonderful sense of humor. Your candor keeps me on my toes and I am fortunate to be your Mom.

To all the fantastic women that I know and those that I haven't met: May your relationships be peppered with enough quirks and idiosyncrasies to discover the funny side.

Mommalogues

**White Bird
Publications**

Yelp Me, Momma

My mom and I were having lunch when she left me mid-conversation. She had that far-away look in her eyes, the one usually reserved when spotting seventy percent off on the clearance rack. "Mom, I was saying..."

"What does that mean?" she asked, pointing at a sign on the restaurant counter. I turned around, knowing I had been dismissed. I read it to her out loud, a habit brought on by having a three-year-old. "If you are not satisfied with our service, please see the manager before you Yelp."

"I can read, dear. What is Yelp?"

"People can write reviews on Yelp using their smartphones. It's a way to evaluate restaurants, businesses—most public places."

"I don't see the point."

I reached for my phone on the table and gave her a quick run through. "See, if you have a great experience, you can let others know. Imagine all the publicity a business gets by having real-time reviews. I've found our little lunch place, and I'm giving it four stars because the waitress has not only been attentive, she gave you enough sugar packets to put your diabetes in overdrive."

"I asked her to do it."

"Yes, and she did. Thus, the four stars."

"And if she hadn't?" I could see the cogs turning in Mom's mind.

"Then, they might get a bad review."

"Hmmm."

I immediately regretted my reply. Yelp could turn

out to be yet another complaint vehicle for senior citizens. Didn't they have enough in their arsenal?

Two weeks later, I went to pick up Mom from her bridge game. She usually waits for me out front. Same bench under the elm tree. Like clockwork. I gave her fifteen minutes, and when she didn't come out, I went to find her. The cards were apparently an afterthought, as I saw Mom with six other ladies around her, smartphones in hand. What were they...?

Mom said, "Rate it, and hit send." Then, I knew. A crash course in Yelp. Who knew a harmless sign in a restaurant would unleash the newest form of entertainment for the bridge gals?

"Dear, what are you doing here? I always meet you out front," Mom said, with the same tone of innocence as my young daughter.

"It's time to go." I tried giving the others an apologetic smile, but their heads were bent, their fingers fumbling over their phones. "I'm double-parked."

The setback at the Senior Center meant we would be late for her doctor appointment. After signing in and taking a seat, Mom said, "You know, I found that restaurant that your father and I went to on our thirtieth anniversary."

"Found it? The one in New York?"

"Yes. I looked it up and gave it a review. I Yelped it," she said, a look of pride washing over her face.

"Mom, that was ten years ago." I started to feel a little queasy.

"I know, but I never did like the booth where we sat. It was very noisy. Very distracting. They should just remove it altogether."

"You Yelped that?" I didn't realize I had raised my voice until a couple of people looked at me.

"That's not all. Our waiter, Carlo, was rude. He gave the other table more attention than your father and I. And, he forgot to refill my water glass."

"Carlo? You can't remember to take out your trash every week; yet you remember a Carlo from a decade ago?"

"Carlo is the name of your second cousin's husband's brother. And it was a very warm evening so, of course, I would remember the lack of water."

I silently counted to three, another little jewel of patience honed from my daughter, before saying,

"This is not what Yelp was intended for. I mean, you can't go back decades."

"Suit yourself, but I'll do it my way." Her newly found smugness was a little disarming.

"Mom, there's a statute of limitations on complaining."

"State of nations?"

"Stat-ute of lim-i-ta-tions," I answered. Add hearing aid check-up to the list of appointments in her future. "It means that there's a logical time frame, like within the last year. You have to be current. I thought I made that clear."

"No, you didn't." She was quiet a minute before saying, "Then I probably shouldn't have Yelped Madison Square Gardens."

"You haven't lived in New York for thirty-five years!"

"All the same, my experience wasn't a good one."

"That's because you disliked your date."

We were saved any further conversation when the nurse escorted us to a room, and the rheumatologist walked in. He asked Mom to describe her symptoms.

"The joints in my hands hurt. A lot. Especially in

the morning."

"Maybe it's your Yelping muscles?" I offered.

The doctor gave me a blank look. My mom gave me the look that told me to back off.

After a brief exam, the doctor decided to change her arthritis medication. I thought all was well until we reached the check-out desk. Mom went to use the ladies room, leaving me to turn in the final paperwork.

The nurse handed me a brown bag filled with samples of Mom's new medication. Her direct eye contact never wavered as she said, "Please make sure your Mom gets these. She mentioned something about Yelping, and we want her to be happy."

Once inside the house, my young daughter came rushing down the stairs to greet us. I had no sooner walked into the kitchen to start dinner when I heard her sweet voice. "Gramma, would you please read me a story? I've had a bad day."

"You went to pre-school. How bad could that be?" Mom said.

"They ran out of snacks and lost my favorite toy."

"That's too bad, honey," Mom said.

"And, the wheels on the scooters are really

wobbly. I crashed and got this boo-boo on my knee."

"Before we read, would you be a dear and hand Gramma her cell phone?"

Donna Todd

Skype, Skype, Baby

The computer beeps, and my daughter comes running, better trained than one of Pavlov's dogs. It is Sunday night, almost seven-thirty in the evening and she knows who will be there. Gramma. It has been this way for the last month, since my mom decided that she needed to end the weekend being on Skype with her granddaughter. Even though we only lived five miles apart.

"Hi, Gramma," she coos. "I knew it was you."

"Hi, Mom," I said. I tried explaining before that Skype was mainly used for business meetings, interviews, and out-of-the-area chats where you needed to see each other live, but she would have none of it. Clearly, I was misled.

"How are my favorite girls?"

"We're fine..." I stopped mid-sentence, noticing that Mom was awfully close to the monitor and had make-up on, complete with sangria-colored lipstick. "You're all dolled up."

"Yes. It's for my performance." She took several steps back, and I saw the side of a stage and some high-backed stools.

"Where are you, and what are you doing?" She usually sits in her recliner, laptop perched on her legs.

"I'm going to do karaoke, and I want my granddaughter to see."

"Karaoke?" I got that sinking feeling in the pit of my stomach that I get whenever one of my kids wants to try something dicey. How had my Mom transitioned from singing songs from Barney and reminding my daughter to wash her hands before meals to this? In just one week's time? I knew I should have paid more attention when she took that flyer from the restaurant. I took a deep breath. "What are you going to sing?"

"It's a surprise," she said, a big grin on her face.

"No, Mom. I'm pretty sure karaoke is the surprise."

"Well if you must know, it's *Girls Just Wanna Have Fun*. It's by Cyndi..."

"Lauper," I said. A song from my era. A rite of passage song, an anthem for the time. "Mom, it was cool back when, you know; it was for me and my friends."

"Oh, now, don't be a killjoy."

Before I had a chance to say another word, we watched in amazement as my mom's hot pink dress came into full view. Gone were the sensible loafers, replaced with shiny, white pumps. I'm certain my mouth made a complete 'O' shape when I saw the pink boa scarf wrapped around her neck.

"Wow." My daughter exclaimed.

"Yeah, wow," I echoed.

"Gramma's gonna sing; gramma's gonna sing."

The introduction to the song started, and Mom took her place on the stage, facing the monitor, ready for her first note. I took a deep breath as three of her friends from the bridge club hobbled as fast as they could to join her, also in pink, the color du jour.

My daughter grabbed a pencil to use as a microphone, and I sat down to steady myself. Uncanny that my little girl had never heard the song before but could easily belt out the 'Girls Just Wanna Have Fun' chorus. Like I had. And my friends. And so many others before and after us. Over three decades ago.

So right there, in the security of my kitchen, I watched Mom and three other gals whose collective age was greater than two hundred-eighty years, perform a flashback to the eighties. I looked around, praying my husband didn't walk in the room. He didn't need any more fodder for the mother-in-law mill.

To my disbelief, they were good. Not practiced-for-hours good. Not take-it-on the road good. But they were holding their own. My mom, lead vocalist, twirled her scarf around for emphasis, and her friends followed. They were smiling, looking years younger, and having a blast.

"I love it!" My daughter shrieked.

When the song ended almost four minutes later, the applause was deafening. Busboys and tired waitresses had gathered around, cheering for Mom-plus-three. The guy who ran the karaoke machine came and kissed each one on the cheek, telling them they were welcome back. Anytime.

Mom came rushing into view, her jubilant face filling the monitor screen, to say good-night.

"Gramma, that was the best. The very best."

"Thank you, dear. Remind your Mom that Skype isn't just for overseas chats." She gave a smug grin. "It's to keep us connected."

"Great job, Mom. Cyndi would be proud." We said our good-nights, and I wondered if Mom would sing another. And if she did, we would miss it.

An hour later, as Cyndi's catchy verse, sung Mom-style, was still stuck in my head, I walked into my daughter's room to tuck her in. She had already fallen asleep; her golden hair spread out like a fan on the pillow. In her hand was her pencil microphone. On her nightstand were three Barbie dolls, each one dressed in pink.

Paint it Red

I've discovered that whenever I take my mom shopping, she conveniently disappears on me. It most often happens around ten minutes in, but today she hit the five-minute mark. She wandered off, and 'poof,' she has pulled a Houdini, leaving me to figure out where she has gone. I'd like to think it's her way of exerting some independence and not her payback for my short-lived-but-infuriating rebellious teen streak she likes to remind me about. Today, I decide against trying to figure out her motive and continue shopping in the produce aisle. At least I can shop in peace and not have to bribe her with candy bars like my kids. Twenty minutes pass before I decide to text her. Here is Mom's reply: *Next door. At the nail salon. Getting a pedicure.*

The only people to ever touch my mom's feet were the podiatrist that removed a bunion last year and my three-year-old daughter who is allowed to paint Mom's nails. She sits patiently as her granddaughter, the nail artist, not only colors the nail bed, but the surrounding skin on her toes. When my daughter leaves, Mom covertly fixes it with polish remover.

"I never would have guessed that this is where you would be," I said, entering the salon after putting the groceries away. I smiled at the receptionist, who knows me from previous visits.

"Really?' Mom asked, in a tone that indicated that she knew damn well that I would be surprised.

"Yeah, Mom. Really."

"Well, I overheard these two young gals talking at

the coffee shop, and they said something about telling a person's age by whether or not they get pedicures. That old people don't do it."

She shrugged her shoulders and grinned at the gal massaging her feet. "I just bought a new pair of sandals. And I definitely don't want to be thought of as old. More importantly, we are getting acquainted. My gal Jenny here is a fantastic conversationalist."

Jenny smiled. I waited for her add something more, but she didn't. Instead, she nodded her head before walking to the back of the salon.

I leaned forward and said, "She doesn't understand a word you are saying."

Mom looked like I had just thrown cold water in her face. "What? No. You're wrong." She looked around the place, sizing it up.

I did the same, wanting to see if from a beginner's lens, just like her. All around us clients were engaging in monologues. No two-way exchanges were happening. "Sorry, but I'm right."

"I was talking about my garden, and she asked about a flower."

"A flower? She didn't mean from a garden; she was upselling. Probably one of the few English phrases she learned on training day. She wants to paint a flower on your big toe and charge you for it."

"But I told her all about my..."

"Trust me; she doesn't have a clue."

Minutes later, Jenny appeared with a steaming towel in her hand. She sat down on the stool in front of Mom's chair, blotting her feet.

"You know," I said, making direct eye contact with Jenny, "my mom makes the most delicious casseroles using Kibbles and Bits. With a furball crust."

Jenny gave another smile, robotic-like, all the while scrubbing Mom's heels.

Mom gave me a sidelong look. I slowly nodded, as we both tried to keep a straight face. Not the time for an I-told-you-so, but I didn't have to go there. Mom read my expression.

Just as I thought the point had been made, Mom went for the daily double. She leaned forward and lowered her voice as if telling Jenny a playground secret. "I was digging in my garden last week, and I found a corpse in my back yard. Only to remember that I buried it there ten years ago."

"That nice," Jenny answered.

I bit my lip to keep from bursting out loud, our conspiracy now complete. Jenny patted my mom's feet one last time before reaching for two jars of nail polish. "Which color for you?"

"The Ruby red one, please," Mom said, tapping the bottle to make sure she understood. She had lost her sense of kinship with Jenny, but I owed it to Mom to set her straight. And we gained a little camaraderie.

Jenny finished the job in silence, most likely thankful that Mom had not engaged her in anything else she did not understand. I refused to make eye contact lest Jenny figure out that we were on to her.

After the bill had been paid, Jenny escorted Mom to an area of the salon to let her nails dry, setting a fan down on the floor in front of her.

Moments later, Mom took out her cell phone and took a picture of her feet.

"A foot selfie?" I asked. "Now I've seen it all."

Mom shrugged. "A memory of my first and last pedicure."

"Really?" I asked. Next time she wandered off, I could omit nail salon from her list of hiding places.

"Yeah," Mom stood and reached for her handbag. "Let's get out of here. Jenny seems to be a very nice gal, but from now on, I'm sticking with my granddaughter. At least she understands me."

Day Tripper

I didn't know that a field trip for my six-year-old son was going to span three generations. I had agreed a month in advance to accompany his class to the museum. When another parent got sick at the last minute, the teacher invited my mom in her place.

"Didn't you have enough of these trips when we were kids?" I asked Mom when she arrived at school, hoping she might reconsider. "I mean, you'll miss your morning game shows. And The View. Is it really worth it?"

"Of course, dear. Please don't give me that discouraging tone. Besides, I DVR'd my programs. I'm good to go."

"You'll be in a different group than us," I said, pointing to where my son stood with his friends. He came over and gave his gramma a hug.

"That's okay. We'll sit together at lunch." She patted his head before he returned to wait for the bus.

Because the teacher had the foresight to remind the kids that their Friday afternoon Popsicle party would be canceled if they misbehaved on the bus, we had a quiet and uneventful ride. Once inside, the docent read off the standard rules—no touching, running, or loud talk was permitted. We were then divvied up, with each group going to a different room in the museum.

My jaw dropped when I saw my mom leave with three boys trailing reluctantly behind her. I figured the teacher wanted the morning off when she assigned herself the calm kids and gave Mom the trifecta of bad behavior.

Fifteen minutes into the presentation, my kids were doing just fine, so I peeked around the corner at my mom. I took a quick intake of air as I saw one boy scooting around, wiping the floor with his bottom, another one practicing what looked like a baseball slide toward an imaginary base and the third one standing on a small bench, balancing on one leg as he acted out the pose of the sculpture next to him. To my disbelief, the docent continued talking in a monotone voice while Mom bent over and reached under the little Swiffer's armpits to pull him upright. He was giggling, reveling in attention of any kind.

Once Mom had him on two legs, she headed for the bench and demanded the other boy break pose. When he didn't comply, she pointed vehemently toward the floor and gave him the stink-eye. He moved off the bench and attempted to trip the slider. The kid who had been floor mopping, then, gave him a push.

I walked to the other side of the room where I could get a look at the teacher. She was deep in conversation with the docent while her little angels listened patiently. Thankfully, my room separated them so she wouldn't see the boys misbehaving and Mom's attempt to rein them in.

At that very moment, a shrill sound went off in Mom's area. I turned and noticed that my son went to check it out. His face turned white. "Gramma set off the alarm," he whispered. I came over just as the guard approached the group.

"Did one of you boys get too close?" He said accusingly. He walked to the far wall to turn off the alarm.

Mom's long index finger was pointing to something on the canvas. "They did not."

"What are you doing?" I hissed under my breath.

"Ma'am, don't touch that painting," the guard said in a very stern tone.

"I wasn't touching it," Mom said. "I would never do that."

The boys had completely stopped goofing around. Mom had made their behavior look acceptable, and they were claiming this moment.

"You're standing too close," the guard said.

"That's why the alarm went off."

"I'm sorry," Mom said. "I was demonstrating how this artist used layers to appeal to the sensory of touch when creating her collage."

"You must do that without any contact," he said.

The boys remained silent, curious as to how Mom would handle this *faux pas*. So was I. She took a step back but kept her pointer in the air as she continued. "See, boys, I was showing you how she could have put a cone on a canvas and called it a day. Instead, she interconnected additional cones to create a 3D effect."

The threesome became very interested in her description. The guard settled down a bit, still keeping a nervous stance, ready to spring back into action.

"If you look closely," Mom said, "she used sand, paint, and steel for the effect."

"It looks like paint from a can," said Baseball slider.

"Very good. She used a combination of spray paint, emulsion, and acrylic."

"Wow! I didn't know you were smart." Swiffer said.

Just as I thought Mom might take offense, she surprised me.

"Thank you, young man. I'll tell you something. I was a volunteer here long before you were ever born. I met the artist who created this collage."

"Cool," he answered, while the others nodded their heads. Clearly, Mom had surpassed the docent's two bullet points on this artist.

"You best get back to your group." Mom motioned toward my room.

"Just making sure that everything is all right," I said sweetly.

Mom looked at the docent. "I think we're done here. Shall we proceed to the Renaissance room where we can show these young scholars the early Cezanne painting?" Mom started to leave, and the notorious three followed in a line so straight I visualized them tethered to an imaginary rope. Like a mama duck leading her babies they continued, the docent, bringing up the rear, the guard walking back to his original position near the doorway.

An hour later, our tour was finished. We walked

to the picnic benches to join the class for lunch.

"Nice going, Mom. Way to turn it around."

"Thank you, dear."

"Once again, I learned something new. You were once a docent?"

"Yes. And our gal today was noticeably inexperienced. They really ought to give her more training. Her delivery was as exciting as watching paint dry. Pun intended."

Before we could find our places to sit, the teacher came rushing over. "Would you be available for our Mission trip on the 23rd of next month?"

"Sure," I said.

"Oh, okay," the teacher paused a second. "You can come, too. I just wanted to make sure that Gramma could join us. I have three boys who requested to be in her group again."

Donna Todd

Magical Mystery Tour

The favor of giving my Mom a ride to the store took a complete detour, one I never saw coming. When I arrived to pick her up, I didn't even have a chance to get out of the car, as Mom locked the front door and came to greet me. Her hair was pulled back, and she'd skipped the lipstick. My eyes quickly trailed down to her legs.

"Good morning," she said, hopping inside the car,

wearing red microfiber pants with scottie dog graphics on them, tucked into a pair of Ugg boots.

"Morning," I replied. "I didn't get the memo about pajama day," I said, pointing to my jeans.

"This is loungewear, dear. Don't all you busy moms know about it?"

"Yes, I've heard the term. But I'm pretty sure it's reserved for solid colors." I backed out of the driveway.

"Have it your way. This will add to the authenticity."

"Authenticity of what?"

"We're going to the mall. Today, I'm a mystery shopper."

"What? I thought...the grocery store. Oh great. Now you're dragging me along to witness your harassment of a minimum wage worker."

"It's not harassment. It's their opportunity to dazzle. Besides, this is an upscale department store where the clerks get commissions. They make more than minimum wage."

"How long have you been doing this?"

"Almost a year."

"And this is the first I've heard of it? You tell me every time your knee acts up. You gave me explicit details about your last root canal, but you omit this?"

"I'm sure you don't tell me everything. Usually, I take one of my gals from the bridge club. Now please, drive around and get a spot out front."

"I know where to go." I glanced over at Mom, who had gone quiet. She had pulled out a sheet of paper from her purse and was reading it.

"You should have been specific about where I was taking you," I said. "I don't like being ambushed. I feel like an accomplice."

"Such negative words. Try replacing them with checklist and backstory."

"Why?" I ask, deciding to play along.

She waved her paper in the air. "These are the guidelines I must follow. To make sure everything is done properly. And the backstory is mine."

"Yeah, I'll bet," I said.

"That sounds sarcastic, and I'm going to ignore it. Every mystery-shopping professional worth their salt comes in with a little backstory, lest the clerk spots an imposter. This will be fun."

"Watching you perform in community theater was fun—sort of. Are you sure we shouldn't just go home? I promise to take you to audition for the next play."

"Well, I'll certainly be able to use some of my acting skills."

We entered and headed for the second level. Women's casual and dressy attire. I wondered what criteria would deem this a successful event and hoped for all our sake that the salesperson could deliver. Our girl Roxi introduced herself moments after we stepped off the elevator. I knew she was a good poker player because after she had looked at my Mom's loungewear, she was able to keep a straight face.

"Are you shopping for a special event today?" Her youth and enthusiasm were sure to get her some points on Mom's secret list.

"Yes, she is," I said, touching my Mom's shoulder. "She needs a dress for a bris." I paused for a moment, certain she didn't know what I was talking about, before adding, "it's where they chop the foreskin from an eight-day-old baby's penis."

Mom elbowed me in the side, and her impact landed right between my ribs.

"Oh. Is this your usual style?" Roxi asked Mom, taking in her get-up for the second time.

"My usual style?" Heavens, no. Just because I opted for a casual look doesn't mean you should assume I would wear this to a...a bris," Mom answered.

"I...it's something I always ask. To see if there's a particular look you like," Roxi said.

"Perhaps you should assess the situation before asking," Mom said. There were sure to be a few red marks on that checklist now.

"Just a nice all-occasion dress will do," I said, giving Mom my best backstory wink. "Isn't that what you told me on the way over?"

"Yes, dear," Mom said, shooting me the look. The one that said I had hijacked her story, she was irritated at the salesgirl, and one more comment would be taking it too far.

"Maybe something cheery, colorful?" Roxi asked. Now we both had to stifle laughter.

Five minutes later, my Mom entered the dressing room with three dresses to try on, compliments of Roxi, who went back up in my estimation. Three was the number I used when giving my kids a choice. Anything more than that and a stalemate was sure to happen.

The first dress was black with a high white collar. I watched Mom look in the three-way mirror. "If you put your hair in a bun you'll look like Olive Oyl," I said. "Next."

True to her suggestion, Roxi had thrown in a bright floral A-line number. As Mom came out to show me the second choice, I shook my head. "Maria from *Sound of Music*—after she falls for Captain Von Trapp. You know, Mom, you don't really have to try these on. She'll never know."

"Now, how can I write a decent report if I don't complete the shopping experience? I take my mystery shopping duties seriously."

My stomach gave a little rumble, and I looked at my watch. It was past lunchtime. "Try on the last one, then."

The third selection was the best. A simple navy dress cinched at the waist with a white belt. "I like it," I said.

"Not too old-school airline attendant?" Mom asked.

"No."

Roxi came by one last time. I'm certain she was relieved when the woman in the doggie pajamas/loungewear had made a decision. She told us she'd meet us at the counter to ring up the purchase.

The place was getting busy, and I noticed a few of the couture women eyeballing Mom's attire.

"Well, one more job completed," Mom said as we walked toward the elevator.

The smells wafting from the café in the rear of the store tempted me. "Let's get lunch," I said.

"I really should go home and write my report," Mom said.

"Just a quick bite, my treat. On one condition."

"What is that?"

"That you never take me on a mystery shopping trip again," I said.

"Okay, you've got it. My friends would never upstage my backstory."

"Make that two."

"What else?"

"The next time you get the urge to dress like you're going to a Polar Express party, you call one of your bridge gals."

Baby, You Can Drive My Car

Upcoming birthdays are usually a time for celebrating with cake and presents. In my mom's case, it was a prompt for the dreaded Department of Motor Vehicles license renewal.

Her call came right after a work meeting ended. "I know you're busy," she said, "so I'll cut to the chase. I have my DMV renewal, Friday at four. Both the written and the driving part. Can you go with me?"

"Take you? To pass a driver's test?" Did she hear

how ludicrous it sounded?

"For the moral support."

I took a deep breath. I knew there was a great deal of stress around this appointment, and my dad would take her when he was alive. "Okay. I'll do it. I'll pick you up."

"Oh no, dear. I'll come get you. I need the practice."

My mom arrived forty-five minutes early on Friday. I was folding laundry when she texted me to let me know she was outside. Irritated that she wouldn't get out of the car and knock, I texted back my reply: *Give me a few minutes. Study your handbook.*

When I walked outside, Mom's head was pressed against the headrest; her eyes were closed, and she was listening to one of her political shows on the radio. I got inside the car and pointed to the DMV pamphlet on the console. "You should be looking at it."

"I already did. Listening to the radio relaxes me." She started the ignition, and we very slowly backed out of the driveway. My mom has two speeds: slow and slightly erratic. There is no middle ground. Dad had the patience of Job to endure driving with her. Since this wasn't the time to offer any constructive criticism, I silently hoped that her instructor would be in an accepting frame of mind. I turned the radio off and grabbed the book, flipping through the pages.

"Okay," I said, "First question. Roadways are the most slippery: A: During a heavy downpour, B: After it has been raining, or C: The first rain after a dry spell?"

"What temperature is it? How windy is it?" Mom asked.

"What does it have to do with the question?"

"Variables. They affect everything."

"Just answer."

"Let me think," Mom said. "I drove with Maude early last winter when we had that brief but monsoon-like rain. She swerved, and I swear, I thought we were going to hit the car in the other lane. It was a pretty red Mustang, too. The wheels on Maude's car..."

"Mom, there isn't an essay section on the DMV test."

"I'm employing deductive reasoning."

"You should have studied and memorized it. It's one of three possible answers which means you have a thirty-three and a third percent chance of getting it right."

"Those aren't bad odds," Mom said.

Was this really how I was kicking off the weekend? "Flip it. You have over a sixty-six percent chance of being wrong if you just wing it."

"Oh." She went silent for a moment, never taking her hands of the ten-and-two position on the steering wheel. That ought to gain her some points.

"My answer would be the last one. The one about the dry spell."

"Correct." Would she pull it off after all?

Mom turned into the crowded parking lot. We circled around, trying to locate a space as she hovered over the brakes, slamming them hard as she edged her way around the parking lot. If they had a candid camera eyeing the lot, she was doomed. I jolted along the first couple of times until I couldn't stand it any longer. "Stop riding the break. You'll wear out the pads. Not to mention you'll give your instructor whiplash."

"I only break when it's necessary."

"You're an over-breaker. You even do it when I'm the one driving. You imaginary break; don't think I don't notice. You've been doing it since I had a learner's permit," I said.

A spot became available, and she parked. The place was swarming with people. Good to know that the government tedium was in full swing. Thank goodness for the appointment system because Mom was called right away and escorted to a private room to take her exam. Fifteen minutes later, she successfully passed and advanced to the eye test. Of course, she had to rummage around in her purse for her eyeglasses, and just when I thought this part was going to be a bust, she pulled them out from deep within a side pocket, a gum wrapper stuck to the eyeglass chain.

The tired worker behind the counter actually looked up at the clock. I couldn't blame him. Quitting time was almost here. He asked the standard read-and-cover each eye questions, recording the paperwork.

He pointed to rows of hard, plastic chairs. "The

next part is behind the wheel. An instructor will come get you."

We waited together until a middle-aged woman with a severe bun appeared and called Mom's name. Her lipstick was a little too bright, and I couldn't get a read on her. I felt like I did on my son's first day of preschool. That anxious feeling in the pit of your stomach while silently praying for a positive outcome. I wished I could take the test for her.

I tried to settle into one of those horrid chairs but was fearful of touching the armrest. Unrecognizable grime covered the surface. Twenty-five minutes later, which seemed like an eternity, but only a blip in DMV minutes, Mom walked back inside, waving a piece of paper. She smiled, saying, "I passed. Thank goodness this is over."

"How did you do?" I asked.

"Well, she docked me for an unsafe lane change..."

"Oh, that's all? She wasn't into a potential side-swipe? Picky, picky." My shoulder muscles relaxed a bit.

"She mentioned something about an early birthday present and told me to always drive defensively. Honestly, I don't think I deserved the ding. I did it exactly like the booklet stated. I signaled, checked my mirror, and then went."

"How about your blind spot?"

She shrugged. "The other drivers need to take some responsibility. I signaled for intent, not permission."

I sighed and took my place back in the chair while she went to the photo station. The line was the longest Mom had encountered so far. I wished I would have remembered to bring my Kindle.

I used the time to check work e-mails. I was lost in replies when Mom's text message flashed at the top of my phone. *I need you. Hurry.*

What now? Surely, she hadn't forgotten some important piece of paperwork. Getting her picture taken was the last hurdle, and I was ready to go. Mom stood on the spot with the blue background behind her, holding up a long string of people waiting in line.

"What do you need?" I asked.

"Let me borrow your sweater," she said.

"You texted me for that?"

"I'm wearing white. This won't be a good driver's license picture. I'll look washed out."

"You have got to be kidding," I said, taking off my coral colored sweater. I rolled it in a ball and handed it to her. A woman was glaring at us. "I'll be in the car."

When Mom returned and got inside, she laid my sweater on my lap. "Thank you, dear. And for coming here today. One more stop, and I can drop you off."

"Take me home first."

"Just a quick detour to the bus depot. Today is the last day of the month, and I need to get my monthly pass. You know I prefer to use public transit."

Horizon Line

Occasionally, my Mom gets in one of her mother/daughter bonding moments. Usually, that means a trip to the mall followed by either lunch or a Frappucino. Sometimes, both. So, I was surprised when she called me the evening before with a change of plans.

"Let's do something different," Mom said. "I've got this Groupon for kayaking. It's in La Jolla Cove."

"You're kidding?" I silently cursed Groupon under my breath. "You realize it takes a lot of upper body strength." A trip to Costco with her usually counted as my arm workout for the day as I helped haul her groceries inside the house.

"I've been going to the gym. I've got this. See you in the morning, and don't forget sunscreen."

The traffic was light, so we made the drive down the freeway in under an hour. The Pacific Ocean sparkled, and several boats dotted the horizon. When we arrived at the check-in, we were greeted by a handsome young man with dark hair and a laid-back style. His name badge read: Kane.

"Welcome ladies," he said, taking the paper tickets my Mom had printed. "Do you want your own kayak or do you need a double?"

"Share?" Mom said.

"My own," I said. We spoke at the exact same moment, so Kane was confused.

"I think it would be fun," Mom said.

"I don't." I had a quick flashback to the time we rode a tandem bike together. It was a long time ago, but the memory of trying to get in sync as the winds kicked up was still cemented in my brain. I shook my head. "My own, please."

Kane handed us some vouchers. "Go ahead, and wait with the others until we head out to the ocean."

Mom and I walked to the waiting area. She looked tense. "Did he say the ocean?" She whispered. "I thought we were kayaking in a cove."

"Did you think we would be airlifted and dropped there? We paddle to it."

"Ocean kayaking is different from the lake," Mom said. "I've only been on calm waters. I'm entering the waves of the Pacific on a two-by-four."

"It's mind over matter. Come on; it's time to go." We walked with the group for five minutes. True to Mom's concern, the vast Pacific, a blanket of salty water, was our entry point. One lone boat, far out on the horizon, cast a silhouette against the blue sky. I tried to cheer Mom up by pointing south, toward the cove.

Two more equally handsome, dark haired guys appeared to help Kane. He introduced them. "Meet your other guides. The guy in the blue trunks is Keoni, the one in the orange trunks is Pele."

Did he really just say Pele? Our safety would be guarded by three guys who most likely left food service jobs in the Hawaiian Islands to work on the mainland. They all had straight, white teeth and tan bodies. They removed their shirts and started helping the group assemble their equipment. Add six-pack abs to the list.

"You go before me," Mom said under her breath, "and then paddle out and wait for me. I'll follow."

"Fine." I had to admit I had a little trepidation about being in the ocean, mainly because I didn't want to fall in and try to hoist myself back on a device that weighs about fifty pounds while waves slapped at my bottom.

Keoni motioned me forward, so I got in the kayak and immediately paddled in a high angle motion to slice my way over the small breakers. Muscle memory kicked in, and I quickly caught up to the rest of our group. Taking in the beautiful scenery, I realized Mom was nowhere in sight. I glanced around, back toward the other kayakers. The three Hawaiians were heading this way, so I knew she had left the shore.

An older gentlemen in our group pointed toward a speck on the horizon. "Is that the lady that was with you?" he asked.

Good Lord. I squinted, making out the blue sleeves of Mom's rash guard, extending from her safety vest. She had surpassed us, and it didn't look like she planned on turning around anytime soon. Before I could ask for help, Keoni made his way toward her. We patiently waited while he caught up and gave Mom yet another lesson on making a turn. She was smiling and paddling, enjoying their one-on-one, oblivious to the rest of the group.

"Where were you heading, Ishmael?" I said, once she rejoined us. "Mexico? You told me to wait for you."

"I couldn't help it. I got nervous, so I just kept this darn kayak moving. And now, I have to pee."

"Ease up on the death grip. Your knuckles are white."

We all attempted our strokes in some form of

unity, following the three guys as we navigated the ocean. We had just arrived at the inlet when Mom slammed the bow of her kayak against another, which sent them both flying out of their vessels and into the ocean. As Mom bobbed back to the surface, sputtering salt water, I gave a quick look in Keoni's direction. His Aloha spirit was definitely being challenged. He paddled over to the scene of the crime. Long, muscular arms practically scooped Mom out of the water. She beamed, not in embarrassment, but because she was reveling in the attention.

"Guess there's no such thing as a hit-and-run out here," Mom said as she lifted her body in the kayak and righted herself.

I'd never been so happy to be wearing dark sunglasses because Mom says stupid things when she's uneasy. I leaned toward her. "Let's hear it for those core exercises you've been bragging about."

She gave me a dirty look, and I was thankful her oar wasn't longer. We turned our attention to our guides. For them, this was child's play compared to rowing an outrigger. Kane told us this was our time to take a small break as he narrated about the sea life below and around us. We all reached for a thick piece of seaweed, and some tasted it. Myself excluded since my husband oversalts everything. A couple of sea lions were basking on a large buoy, and it made for a good photo opportunity.

When it was time to head back, we all successfully did our sweep strokes to turn, Mom included, and we made it back to shore without incident.

We returned the oars to the shop and retrieved our personal items from the locker. "Thanks for joining us today," Kane said. "Hope to see you again."

"Now that was fun," Mom said, as we walked to the car and got inside. She pulled a flyer out of her purse. "The nice young man that helped me so much gave this to me. They offer other excursions, and he told me I should try tandem parasailing. He gave me a two-for-one deal."

"Well, you can count me out. I'm staying on terra firma."

"Oh, not you and I." Mom gave a nervous laugh. "I was invited to go as Keoni's guest."

Donna Todd

You've Got a Friend

There was something I needed to tell my mom, but I decided to wait until after dinner. Her disappointment would be digested better on a full stomach. After my oldest had cleared the plates, I sent both kids upstairs to choose their bedtime story. My husband cleared his throat, my cue that I best spill the news.

"Mom, I'm sorry, but I can't go on our trip to the casino next weekend."

"Really?" She had been talking about this for weeks.

Before she could start negotiating like one of my kids, I added, "We have a deadline at work. Everyone in my department has to be there; it's mandatory."

"Oh, dear."

"You should go without me. Invite one of your friends from the bridge club. "

"Oh, those gals aren't the ones you take to Vegas."

"Why not? Invite..." I stalled a minute, trying to drum up some names. "Maude. She seems nice."

"Can't travel with her. She's a hugger."

"What is wrong with that?"

My husband, the king of impeccable timing, rose from the table and excused himself.

"I plan to wear my linen dress. One big hug from her, and I'll look like crepe paper. I'm not walking into Caesar's Palace looking like that."

"You won't invite her because of a few wrinkles?" I'll admit, my husband had his exit strategy down to a science.

Mom added some honey to her tea. "I don't think

she's good in public places for long periods of time. She talks a lot, and she'll even do it when you're in the restroom stall next to her. I mean, who does that?"

I took a deep breath. I knew a refund for the trip was unlikely, so I added, "How about Edith?"

"Can't dine with her. She doesn't cut her bites in proper pieces. And she speaks with her mouth full. I can hardly bear to look at her."

So much similarity to the toddler parties I'd attended lately. "So, she's a finger food only kind of friend?" I asked. "How about the one that hosted your surprise party...Anya?"

"She snores. And she really likes her Stolichnaya, so, of course, that won't work."

"You've actually heard her snore?"

Mom shrugged which made me feel bad. I knew she was excited about going so I tried another angle. "You taught me that there were different kinds of friends for different kinds of activities." I thought about the people I knew. The introverts were great for going to the movies with. So were the complainers. The brutally honest ones I took shopping, thereby avoiding a fashion *faux pas*. The competitors were my tennis partners.

"Did I really teach you that?"

"You did."

"Well, when you get older the list shrinks a bit."

She had a point. Now that I'd become a busy Mom, acquaintances took a back seat to true blue girlfriends.

"Gramma, we're ready for our story." My son's voice trailed down from the top of the stairs. Maybe great timing was a hereditary gift from my husband.

Two nights later, I was at Anya's house. Mom's bridge club needed a sub, and she convinced me to go. The mission was two-fold: I would play cards and help her choose the right person to invite to Vegas.

Anya ladled some innocuous looking punch into glasses for us and put out a platter of cheese and crackers. She excused herself a couple of times, and by the third time, I peered into the kitchen and saw her adding shots of Stoli to her drink. Her card playing abilities went downhill after that, because it took her a long time to make a bid.

No one seemed to mind. Edith had helped herself to the lion's share of cheese and crackers, putting more-than-bite-size pieces into her mouth, never coming up for air as she talked with the group. Maude chatted between plays so much I found I couldn't think straight. But they were nice ladies and always made me feel welcome. The evening ended, and I had a headache. I'm pretty sure Anya would have hers tomorrow morning.

Maude gave us each a big bear hug goodbye and thanked me for filling in. Once inside the car, Mom said, "Well? Who do you think I should invite?"

"Sorry, Mom. It's a stalemate. Idiosyncrasies aside, which one would be fun?"

The following Saturday, I picked Mom up and drove her to the Senior Center. A large, ultra-sleek bus was already parked out front. I felt a pang of regret. Mom and I had some fun Vegas memories. I had been so preoccupied with work that I hadn't given Mom's choice a second thought. She got out of the car, and I helped her with her luggage.

"Who's joining you?" I asked.

"Well, I'm not wearing my linen dress..."

"Maude?"

At that moment, she appeared, and Mom outstretched her arms, ready for the obligatory embrace. I did the same.

"You're going to have a great time," I said. A little hugging and some chatter could be overlooked. I think Mom made the right decision.

Behind Maude was a very large suitcase.

"You sure brought a lot of clothes for two days," Mom said.

"Not at all. My clothes are in the small duffel bag. The big one is for my apparatus."

Mom raised one eyebrow.

"My nebulizer in case I need a breathing treatment. Just getting over that nasty cold, but don't worry, doc says I'm not contagious. A humidifier because I never take a chance on that dry desert heat. And of course, my CPAP machine. I simply can't get through a night without it."

Dressed to Thrill

My morning routine was going smoothly, and we were almost out the door when my son came running in the kitchen, my cell phone in his hand.

"Mom, you probably want to see this. What is it?"

I looked down at the text and saw a picture of a nude female mannequin in the store window of my very good friend and shop owner, Kendall. She wrote a caption in capital letters next to it: *I'VE BEEN*

TRYING TO REACH YOUR MOM! SHE ISN'T ANSWERING!

"Come on, get your backpack," I said. The text was a long-distance request for help. "We have to leave. Now."

"But what is it?" My son asked. Kids were relentless when they knew that adults were agitated.

"It's like a giant doll," I said, wondering who had sent Kendall the picture. She was on vacation in the Bahamas, and whenever she leaves town, she asks my Mom to work in her boutique.

I dropped my son off and then dialed Mom's cell phone. No answer. I sent a text. Nothing. I let out a long sigh. I drove two miles across town, knowing I was going to be late for work. When I arrived at La Donna's, an upscale shop on the corner of a picturesque square in the downtown area, mannequin lady was still undressed, arms upright in the air, like she was playing volleyball.

The middle school was a block away, and a group of young boys walked by, giggling as they glanced in the window. They all pulled out their phones and took a picture. Apparently, my son wasn't the only curious one. Another took a selfie, outstretching his arm to make it look like he was groping her breast. Boys.

The shop door was open, but Mom wasn't at the front counter. Where the heck was she?

The lady who works at the bakery next door poked her head outside. "It's been this way all morning. Your Mom just left the display that way last night and went home. It's pretty tacky."

A-ha. The text sender. "Thanks for letting me know."

"Kendall runs a classy place. I felt I had to tell her."

Didn't she have some bread to knead or pie crusts to roll? A couple more boys walked by and snickered. "I'll find her," I said, making a vow to order future cakes from another bakery.

I stepped inside the doorway and headed toward the back of the store. "Mom."

"Oh, my! You scared the heck out of me. What are you doing here?"

"There's a mannequin that needs to be dressed."

Mom wore a knit sweater dress, textured black leggings, and taupe boots. She accented it with large, gold hoop earrings, a long necklace and about a half-dozen bracelets on each wrist. All compliments of LaDonna's.

"What's this? You should be dressing the mannequin instead of yourself."

"I was getting to that. But all savvy salespeople know you sell more if you wear the clothes."

"No offense, but I'm pretty sure a properly dressed mannequin will boost sales, too. I will say, great choice on the leggings. Not every woman can pull them off."

"Thank you, dear." She walked to the showroom, and I followed. "If you want a pair, they're over in the Vietnamese section."

I looked around the store and noticed that all the displays had been moved. The interior was hardly recognizable. "What section?"

"Vietnam. I rearranged the store yesterday according to where the clothes come from."

"You're kidding?" In the core of my being, I knew

she wasn't.

"Different countries have different pattern sizes. Before you poo-poo me, hear me out, because I'm on to something. It's the reason why it's possible for me to be a size small in one country and a grande in another."

I felt dizzy thinking about Kendall's face when she came back next week.

"Really, dear, it's a universal problem, and I came up with a solution. Just watch, it's going to be a fashion norm. So, my leggings came from Vietnam, and the sweater dress is from Bangladesh, which is in the way back corner now, as we are just on the brink of cooler weather. My earrings and necklace, a boxed set, are from India. My bracelets are from Sri Lanka." She beamed like she had just invented a cure for cancer. "What do you think about buying little decorative flags from each country to identify each area?"

"Mom, stop! Kendall asked you to help out, not to turn her store into the United Nations." I sure hoped Cupcake Lady next door didn't come inside and tax the memory on her smartphone with more incriminating pictures.

Mom could be relentless when she settled on an idea, and I had a full day's work ahead. I pointed at the tag on one her menagerie of bracelets. "You forgot to remove one of the price tags, Bo Jangles," I said. "And, please, before you go assorting handbags from Ecuador, could you dress the naked mannequin before the store opens? She doesn't make the store very classy."

"Hmmm...there's nothing here from Ecuador..."

"I'm making a point! Just dress her so the puberty-riddled middle schoolers can focus on something else. Naked mannequin has likely made the social media circuit over there, and I don't want it getting back to Kendall."

I arrived at work thirty minutes late, knowing I would shave the time off my lunch hour. I replied to Kendall's text with an upbeat: *All is taken care of. Get some snorkeling in for me!*

The day passed quickly, and the afternoon found me darting back around town, my usual Tuesday routine. When I dropped my son off at soccer practice, curiosity got the best of me. The boutique was only a mile away. I weaved through traffic and found a parking space out front.

Mom waved when she saw me. She walked outside. "Twice in one day? You're spying for Kendall."

I'll admit, I was checking up on her, like I did when I asked my son to clean his room and then circled back to see if it was done. "Can't get anything past you. The window looks great." The mannequin was wearing a very chic indigo tunic, cinched at the waist. Leggings from Vietnam, complete with ankle boots. "What on earth made you undress her in the first place?"

"I didn't like her outfit. The tones clashed. I just knew I could do better." A couple of boys walked by, each with a cell phone in their hands, ready to take a picture. Instead, they looked up at the new display and kept going. Mom chuckled. "I killed their fun by dressing her. Don't think I wasn't on to them."

I looked down the street. A few more boys were heading this way.

"Watch!" Mom said. "It's fun to get inside the display and stand next to her. She could use some company."

"Stop talking like she's real. It's creepy."

Before I could stop her, Mom stepped inside the window and stuck a pose. I watched her limbs go completely still. Her facial expression softened, and her eyes went blank as she stared through the glass to the front of the shop.

She did look pretty good, proving once again, that her theater work was useful. I quickly came to my senses. "Enough, Mom. Get out of there."

She wouldn't answer, and I realized she was waiting for the boys to come by, to see if they would notice. At that moment, Cupcake Lady was closing up shop next door. She looked over, did a quick double take, and reached for her phone, pointing it at the window. Snap.

A customer entered the shop, and Mom was forced to break pose. I received another text from Kendall while Mom was helping the client to a dressing room.

Guess who made it on Facebook?

I sure hoped that wherever she was in the Bahamas, Kendall's cocktail hour had already started.

Donna Todd

Light My Fire

This wasn't how it was supposed to go down. I walked inside my house after a long evening meeting to find my mom and my son sitting at the kitchen table. Whenever she stays with the kids and knows I have put in a full day, she promises to tuck them in so I may return and find my little angels asleep. It's part of the mother/daughter weeknight babysitting creed.

"Hi there," I said, working to keep the irritation

out of my voice.

Apparently, I wasn't successful, because Mom said, "Before you rate the evening as an epic failure, I do have a reason."

"What's that?" I asked, noticing that my daughter had at least made it upstairs. Hopefully, the Sandman was already on his way to her.

"When we went through the homework file," Mom said, "there was one sheet that was unlike the others."

"Gramma helps me clean out my weekly folder, and she lets me throw some of the papers in the fireplace," my son said. "That's my favorite part. I toss the papers inside, and I like to watch the fire gobble up..."

"You use his school papers as kindling?" I asked. The day had just gotten longer.

"Not all the time. Besides, we only toss the unimportant ones."

I felt the pull of a headache starting. What had I missed? Meetings, events, recitals? "How do you know the difference?"

"Oh, dear," said Mom, "I've been through it before. Trust me, if it's really something you need to know, you'll get reminder after reminder. Plus, with all the technology these days, they have a hundred different ways to hound you. The FBI has only slightly better ways of getting to you than the PTA. Tell me, what have you overlooked?"

"How would I know?"

"So I'm actually helping you."

I sat down next to them. Only my mom could circumnavigate a conversation away from why she neglected to get my son to bed and turn it into doing me a favor. It was clear where my children had inherited this trait. And my husband had picked up on it, too.

"Back to your original comment." I pointed to the only paper spared by the fireplace. "What is the problem?"

My son's eyes grew bright waiting for his Gramma to answer, my cue that they had already attempted to go through this together. "This new stuff," she said, flapping the paper in the air. "Common

Core? Are they out of their mind thinking a grandparent can decipher all of the nonsense that comes along with it? I mean, no longer are the kids asked to produce an answer, they must tell exactly how they got the answer. In my day, we practiced our times tables with flash cards."

"It's to help with critical thinking. They're steering away from automatically remembering answers and tying them to concrete concepts."

Mom's mouth formed a tight line. "Now you're sounding exactly like the first paragraph I read. You know how I hate rehearsed speeches."

This could go on indefinitely, especially when Mom wanted to make sure she was right. This might be her ploy to stay on the defense, so I had to play along. "Tell me one of the problems."

"Okay, I will. Three teams of eight are on the field. How many total players are there?

"Twenty-four," my son said, much quicker than he had last week.

"Now for the next part. How did you arrive at that answer?" Mom asked.

"I just did it in my brain. That's how I got it." He gave a triumphant smile.

"Sounds perfectly legit to me, but the teacher told him that wasn't acceptable," Mom answered.

So I offered, "Maybe he should set it up like a word problem?"

"That term is now passé," Mom said with a hint of haughtiness. "They are now called math situations."

"Well, I remember reading that you have to prove these math situations, and there are certain ways to go about it. I just need to find out how." It was coming back, but I was tired; and his homework looked tedious.

As I glanced at all the white spaces on the worksheet, Mom whipped out her phone and dialed. "I'm calling Kendall."

"Not her." Kendall is the one and only parent I know who is on top of everything. The one we're all a bit jealous of because we know it isn't in our genes to be like her. Ever.

"She can help us." Mom hit the speaker button.

"I'm pretty sure she's a robot. Hang up!" Before I

could reach over and hit the disconnect button, Kendall answered.

"Oh, hey, Kendall. I hope I'm not calling too late," I said, scowling at Mom.

"Don't worry about it," she said. "I was just making the kids' lunches for tomorrow. Homemade gluten-free wheat bread. I added some clover honey from my uncle's farm."

I was going to throw together some turkey on week-old rye. "Don't forget the BPA free containers and organic milk," I said sweetly.

"Never. What's up?"

"These math situations, are the kids supposed to prove their answer using some sort of model?"

"Absolutely."

"Such as?"

"Mine like to use number lines or arrays."

My son leaned forward and rested his head on the table.

I immediately went to the computer and googled 'solving math problems using number lines.' I'm sure she heard my fingers clicking away on the keyboard, because she added, "They've offered several workshops on it. The last one was two nights ago. The info came home in the weekly folders."

"Oh, that's right. I had to work late." I narrowed my eyes at my mom as I was forced to tell a little white lie. I'm sure my son registered it and would bring it up at an inopportune time.

"Now, you do know about the PTA meeting tomorrow and the luncheon for Red Ribbon week on Thursday?" Kendall said.

I had absolutely no idea. "Oh, right. Thank goodness for those weekly folders."

"And the book fair. Don't forget that because the kids get to add to their class library."

"I wouldn't dream of it," I said. I thanked her and ended the call before she could verify that I was clueless. It was obvious these events had slipped by me and women like Kendall could sniff through the lies like feral dogs.

"Well?" my Mom asked expectantly.

"You not only threw out the common core sheet but they also held a workshop, and I missed it. That's not all..."

My son jumped in to save her. "We promise not to throw anything away ever again. Okay, Gramma?"

"Sure thing," Mom said, her gaze turning to the fireplace. "Starting tomorrow."

Bingo

Every once in a while, you get to that stage in your mother/daughter relationship where you're thrown a curve. Behavior slightly shifts, and like a stealth fighter, you never see it coming. That's how I felt when my mom, after eating her usual Wednesday night dinner with us, picked up her phone, and after an incessant amount of texting, stated that she needed to leave.

"At least stay for dessert and coffee," I said.

She hastily grabbed her purse, and a couple of lipsticks came tumbling out.

I reached over to pick them up. "Why the rush?"

"Oh, I just have to...you know, I need to...get going." Another chime sounded on her phone.

"Who is texting you? All your friends know that you're having dinner with us."

"Sorry, but I have to go." Mom let out a long sigh. "My services are needed."

"Services?"

"If you must know, I signed on with Lyft."

"What?" I know I said it pretty loud because the dog's ears perked up. "You? Driving people around? You prefer public transit."

"Stop raising your voice and let me explain. The idea came to me because I was constantly giving everyone rides to their doctor appointments. And bingo games. I was asked so often I felt like there was a taxi sign on my car. So I thought, why not Lyft?"

"And I'm thinking, why Lyft? It's so..."

"Controversial? Maybe, but I only accept calls

from my friends. This way, I make a little money and help them, too."

"Heartwarming," I said. "How long have you been doing this?" I felt my eyebrows scrunch into what Mom calls my serious look.

"Long enough to start trending. I noticed a pattern with the bingo players and started recording it. The lucky ones are the ones I like to give rides to. I make sure to pick up their calls when I see their phone numbers because they tip better. I really have to go. This one is from Edith, and she's been lucky her whole life."

I grabbed my handbag and coat. "I'm going with you. I want to see what this is all about." I said good-bye to my husband and kids, promising to do the dishes when I returned.

I was still trying to process Mom's new occupation when we got inside the car. "Don't grammas work in pre-school for extra money anymore?" I asked.

"Not if they want to be a free agent." She backed up, viewing the camera inside the car as she led us down the driveway. I silently thanked the car salesman for bundling the camera in the car purchase. Now that was hindsight.

"What is that smell?" I asked.

"The Cinna-lava-lyptis air freshener? I found that people tip better when I have this smell in the car. Did you know lavender calms emotions?"

"News to me."

Before we headed out of my tract, Mom pulled over and entered the address in her GPS. "I usually do this first thing. Having you here has changed my routine."

"Just drive over to the Senior Center."

Mom ignored me, intent on procedure. Once the address was entered, she took off down the street. We headed in the direction of the Senior Center, but Siri was telling us to make a left three blocks before where I would have turned.

Mom, ever loyal to technology, continued until it was clear we'd passed the area altogether. She made a right turn, and before I could speak, we landed in the parking lot of a strip club. It was in a heavily traveled

L-shaped complex with a laundromat at the far end.

"What? This has got to be wrong." Mom's mouth turned down at the corners.

"You have reached your destination," Siri said.

"Just pick-ups at Bingo, huh?" I asked suspiciously.

"I know that this is Edith's number..." Mom looked in the direction of the club at the man standing outside.

A clean-cut guy, early twenties walked over to the car. He appeared self-conscious when he saw the two of us. "Um...I called for Lyft?"

"Your ride is here," Mom said.

"This isn't your ride," I said. I felt my stomach muscles tighten.

"Don't mind her," Mom said. "Please get inside the car. I can take you to your destination." He ducked in the back seat, and Mom pulled away from the club, turning onto the street.

I firmly placed my right hand on the door handle, ready for a quick get-away if this guy turned out to be a weirdo. What had happened to my mom's judgment?

This from the woman who wouldn't allow me to take a ride from a parent she didn't know. Had she swapped her Mother instinct to make a few bucks?

There was a stretch of silence. I turned slightly so I could get a better look at him, and he caught me.

"I...my buddies took me here. It's my first time, and I'm getting married next weekend."

"Congratulations, young man," Mom said. She kept driving, and he cracked the window slightly, which amused me. Apparently, the lavender mix wasn't working for him, either. It was a short ride to a large apartment complex. When Mom drove around and stopped in front of a building, he looked relieved, yet confused.

"Wait a sec. You knew where to go, and I didn't tell you the building number..."

Mom told him the amount that would be charged to his account. "Do you remember the time we all went to the park, and you fell and broke your arm?' she asked.

His face contorted into a grimace as the realization hit him. "You know my aunt?"

"Don't remember me, huh?" Mom turned around and faced him. "How about the time you and a couple of boys decided to toilet paper Edith's neighbors' house?"

"Oh, yeah. I remember you now." He sighed. "That was a long time ago."

I avoided any further eye contact. It was apparent that he was a victim of Mom's steel-trap memory, of which I had often been a recipient.

He dug in his pockets and held out some bills. "Here's a tip for you."

Mom shook her head. "No thanks. Take the money and buy your fiancée something. Nice to see you again and all the best on your big day."

He had already opened the door and had one leg outside. "Uh, thanks. Good seeing you, too."

"Yeah, I'll bet," Mom said, once he had left. She looked over at me. "And you can let go of that death grip on the door handle."

"That's all you have to say? For the last five minutes, I thought you had gone off the deep end, driving around some millennial whose friends may have left him because he was acting like a creep."

"Have some faith. I recognized him before he walked to my car. He must have borrowed Edith's phone."

"Excuse me for having an overactive imagination." I released my hand. The muscles felt tight, and I massaged the area between my thumb and index finger. "Sure I can't convince you to get a part-time job at the library? Or the florist?" I asked.

Her phone sounded, and she looked at the screen. "I'm needed over at the Senior Center. Anya needs a ride, and some days, she's luckier than Edith. "

Party Wars

When my mom stopped by to pick up some groceries I had purchased for her, I was sitting at the counter, writing tablet open, swiftly making notes.

"What are you doing?" she asked.

"Making plans for your grandson's birthday," I said. I wrote in bold letters across the top of the paper: PARTY THEME.

"But his birthday is a month away."

"I know. I'm already feeling stressed." This would be his first official friend's party. The others were always celebrated with the family.

"What's to stress over?" Mom poured herself a cup of coffee and sat down beside me. "They're seven-year-olds. Call up a couple of his besties, and order a cake. Kids just want to hang out together."

"No phone calls. Evites are sent, and I wait for their responses. Meanwhile, I use the down time to plan up to twenty gift bags. Gone are your days of whipping up a Duncan Hines white cake mix with chocolate frosting and sprinkles."

"I always had Kool-Aid and bowls of potato chips, too," Mom said defensively.

"You wrapped my gift with the funnies from Sunday's paper."

"They were in color, and you loved to read them. What's wrong with that?"

"Nothing." I let out a long sigh, recalling the ink that stained my fingers while opening my present. "You can't get away with hanging some crepe paper streamers and playing a few games. Some of the Moms stay because they want to check out the party, like it's some kind of contest. That or they have absolutely nothing else to do for three free hours. Imagine that. Parties these days take weeks of planning. Add Pinterest, which I'm pretty sure is a synonym for making a working Mom look like a buffoon. There's a reason why I never ventured into this territory before."

"Wait a sec? The Moms stay?"

"Drop-and-runs are looked down upon. If you do it, never admit you're leaving to go somewhere fun, like getting your nails done. It's better to tell the hostess that you're in the middle of house repairs. You'll be completely absolved of any judgment because they'll pity you staying at home and waiting on a repairman."

Mom pointed to the paper. "So what is the theme?"

"Star Wars. Which reminds me, I need to order a costume for him to wear."

"A costume? Good Lord, it's a birthday, not Halloween." She shook her head vehemently from side to side. "Well, I do like Captain Kirk."

These were the times when I noticed the generation gap the most. It wasn't that I couldn't see her point, but I lived in the days of the uber-party and wanted to make it special, make him feel special. "I found a great pinata, so I guess that counts as a game?'

"Not one of those bright colored animals that are made in China? You dangle them from a rope while the kids take turns beating the crap out of it?" she asked.

"Well, yeah, but this one's a Star Wars, R2D2."

"I guess we're lucky it's not a girl party. We'd have tutus, tiaras, tulle, and some sort of butterfly wings to worry about."

I nodded. "Now you're getting the idea."

Mom stood up. "All this nonsense has made me tired. I'm going home. But you can count on me for bringing the cake and helping out." She gave me a hug and left me to assemble the attendee list.

On the big day, my son was so excited he could barely contain himself.

"When will they be here?" he asked, for the tenth time, as I bustled around the house with my *Things to do on the day of the party* list in hand. The morning passed quickly, and by the afternoon my lawn was filled with twenty kids, five of which were drop-offs, leaving me with discriminating Moms. Note to self: next time write Drop Offs Only on the invite.

But they had assembled themselves into their own little groups: The Working Moms, who sat quietly on chairs in the periphery and small talked, the Competitive Moms, who were busy comparing their precocious children, and the Wine Drinking Moms. Their group appeared to be having the most fun, but they weren't watching their kids. Where was my mom anyway? She should have been here by now.

"I just love your decorations and theme," A Wine Mom cooed. "You can't go wrong with Star Wars."

"Thank you," I said, never revealing that I knew next to nothing about Star Wars. Thanks, Pinterest.

The side yard gate swung open, and in walked Mom, clad in her Princess Leia costume. She wore a long, white dress, white boots and had tucked her hair under a brunette wig, parted in the middle with a bun on each side. A light saber was tucked into the side of her belt. Clearly, she'd done her research.

"Hi, Gramma." My son, Luke Skywalker, gave her a hug, eyeing the cake box in her hand. "I like your costume."

"Happy Birthday, sweet boy."

"Yeah, you look cool, like Princess Leia's Mom," said Chewbacca, my son's friend, the socially awkward boy that had been sitting alone on the grass before she appeared. "But you should be carrying a defender-sporting blaster-pistol instead of a light saber."

"Well, Chewbacca, I'm saving up for it." Mom walked into the house, and he followed her.

I quickly looked over at my adult guests to get their gage on Mom's get-up. Most of the attendees were smiling at Princess Leia.

She came back outside just as we lined the kids up for the piñata. My husband had suspended it from an oak tree and was in charge of pulling on the rope to make them look bad when they missed. My son was up first, took a couple of swings, and then his turn ended. A few more boys followed.

A scrawny Darth Vader was next. He took one whack, connected smack in the middle of R2D2, and the candy came pouring out. Kids dove to the ground like vultures, but Darth didn't realize he'd succeeded and gave another hard strike. Before I could react, a white specter of light flashed in front of me as Princess Leia intercepted, grabbing the bat before it connected with another kid's skull.

"You did it," Mom said. "Hurry and pick up some candy."

"Who knew Darth Vader was so strong?" I said nervously.

His Competitive Mom heard me. "Oh, he's been on the swim team since he was two."

"That explains it," I said.

Mom gave me her warning look. "That was a close call. I told you to skip the Chin-ata."

After the candy fiasco, most of the kids moved on to the bounce house. The pizzas were delivered, but none of the kids would sit down at the long, theme-decorated table with name cards that I had assembled. They were like wild animals, darting around the yard, sticking their hands in the candy bowls. My son included.

"This is such a fun party,' said Competitive Mom. "When we did this last year, I had pizzas in the shape of an X-Wing fighter."

When she left, the corners of Mom's mouth turned downward. "X-Wing fighter. Really." She grabbed the pizza cutter and began carving the pizza into bite size pieces. "Give me some toothpicks."

"What are you doing?" I asked.

Chewbacca came over to Mom. "Did you know that Princess Leia was a politician? She was also a revolutionary and the last survivor of the destruction of Alderon."

Mom made a split second decision and handed him a plate. She took the other, and the container of toothpicks. "Come on, Chewbacca." He obediently followed, and we watched as Mom hustled over to the bounce house. She stood in front of it, stabbed each piece of pizza with a toothpick and yelled, "Princess Leia's drive-thru is now open. Come and get your Imperial Pizza! Best in the galaxy!" With that, they stopped jumping and formed a line while she handed them their food.

I walked over to help, checking for the reactions of the Moms in attendance. Most were oblivious. One had a puzzled expression when Princess Leia handed her son a bite, but he devoured it and asked for another.

Mom lowered her voice. "Listen, these kids are eating their weight in sweets; the dog is growling and nipping at Chewbacca's leg, and I'm warding off the dreaded sugar rush, which will save you tears, tantrums, and screaming kids. We have to cram some protein into their little bodies."

I'd witnessed enough party melt-downs to know she was right. If we got through the cake and presents, this day would be considered a success.

An hour later, all the boys had left the backyard, goody bags in hand, except one. Chewbacca.

He was sitting next to my Mom, waiting for his ride. "Did you know, Princess Leia is later revealed to be the twin sister of Luke Skywalker?"

"Really?" Mom asked. My son appeared, dirty and tired, but happy.

"That was so much fun," he said. "You make a good Princess Leia, Gramma."

"Thank you. And because of Wookiepedia here, I know all about her."

Chewbacca smiled and pointed to a gift that had not been opened. "Hey, you forgot one," he said.

My son reached for the package, wrapped in the funnies from the Sunday paper.

Mom winked at me. "With all this new party stuff, I'm keeping with my one tradition."

Let's Get Physical

I've never been one to make a New Year's resolution. I think any time of the year is a good time for self-improvement. Why front-load it all in one month? So when my Mom showed up on January 2nd, wearing the turquoise workout outfit that I bought her three years ago with the price tag still attached to the back of the label, I became suspicious.

She waved a brochure in the air and announced

that she had signed up for a thirty-day trial period at the local gym. My distrust was confirmed when she told me that she had bought one for me as well.

"You can't just do this without asking," I said. My preferred workout was walking the dog and getting away from the chaos of my two kids for thirty minutes. Scooping up warm dog poo in a bag was a small price to pay for the serenity.

"Should I have consulted you for a surprise gift? Plus, it wasn't just me. Your very kind hubby agreed to watch the kids so we can try out some new classes."

Thirty days of togetherness at the gym with Mom? My very kind hubby was going to eat Top Ramen for the next month.

"I've already chosen a few. Have you ever done cardio bar-ray?"

"*Barre*. It's pronounced bar. I've heard of it, but my idea of fun is not group exercise."

"Ignore the others. I intended for these to be healthy mother/daughter outings. You can help me with my New Year's resolution."

"You never keep them. Last year's was to refresh

your Spanish. You spent money on some Rosetta Stone CDs that you never listened to."

"I count weekly conversations with my gardener, Julio, as resolution-worthy."

One hour later, after extracting a future babysitting promise from Mom, I was standing next to her at the waist-high *barre* looking at myself in the mirror. And there were mirrors everywhere. Three-hundred-sixty degrees of myself. No dog, no leash in my hand, or fresh air. Just a room full of mostly-thin ballerina types; give or take a few.

Our long-limbed instructor seemed to flow around the well-lit room with an ethereal presence and encouraging smile. I had to admit, the music tempo was speedier than I anticipated. Before I knew it, I was holding on to the *barre*, doing *releve* with the gusto of my former eight-year-old self, before exchanging ballet lessons for soccer.

Mom was keeping up. I admired her flexibility but only gave a slight nod of my head as we made eye contact, because I still felt roped into this fitness thing. I wouldn't admit it, but I had awakened dormant muscles from my inner thigh down to my ankles as I made the semi-smooth rise up on my toes. And back down again. Up and down, up and down. "This is no joke," I said in between breaths.

"Told you not to quit ballet," Mom whispered.

We transitioned from *releve* to *grand plies*, where we had to turn our feet slightly outward and bend at the knees. I looked at the instructor and copied her. I really felt I had this move down when Mom leaned over.

"You're not doing it right."

"She's bending, I'm bending. In tempo with the music, I might add."

"Your feet are too far apart. Look...her heels are touching. Her plie makes a diamond shape. Yours looks like an A-frame."

There was no time to adjust my position as we were on to the next exercise, which had us backing away from the barre, bending at the waist, and holding on with both hands. My shaky legs were challenged again as I lifted my left leg, pulsed, held it, and balanced it against my own body weight.

"Just five more pulses," the instructor said.

"You're almost there, ladies."

When we were done, I looked over at Mom, leg still in the air.

"I'm stuck. My hip locked." Mom looked at the instructor who was at the other end of the large room. "Unhinge me before she notices."

I've only had to do this once before and not while she was standing flamingo style. I helped her make slow, circular motions until it released.

We finished the rest of the class without incident, and I felt some mystery muscles firing as we left the room.

"Nice job," the instructor said. She smiled at Mom. "In case you're interested, we have a great chair aerobics class that's easy on the joints."

Two nights later, we went to the Senior Strong class. The moment the door opened, members made a beeline to get in position. When Mom placed her chair at the front of the class, another lady shook her head.

"This is my spot," she said. "I always sit here."

Mom gave her the same look she gives me when she's irritated and moved to the right of her. Another head shake from the lady.

"Not here either. That's where my friend likes to sit. She always sits..."

"I wasn't privy to the seating chart." Mom left her chair on the spot and sat down, marking her territory. I placed mine next to her and avoided eye contact with the chair-marker.

Our instructor entered, an alpha-male type named Marcel, who had all the old ladies smiling. We sat down for our warm-up and then moved into sitting abdominal crunches. The music was lively, and after each exercise set, we would get up for a dance routine. His style was high energy as he did arm circles over his head, singing to the music.

Mom was totally into it, singing along with *Ladie's Night.* She broke out a couple hip-hop moves of her own, and I wished we hadn't sat up front. I kept thinking that with the switch- up, the music might stop at any moment—like musical chairs and Mom would be caught in the middle of her Harlem shake.

We decided to continue these two classes for the next four weeks. I never had to unhinge Mom again at

Barre, and she continued her weekly quest to get her place in front at Senior Strong. The tension mounted as Mom and Chair Lady sustained their stand-off. We always arrived early, and Mom chatted with a lot of the members, sans one.

On our last evening there, traffic made us late. We were stopped by the manager when we stepped into the gym. She looked at Mom. "Could you come by the front desk after class? I have a situation I'd like to discuss with you."

"Oh, okay," Mom said.

Once inside, the music had started, and Chair Lady had taken Mom's spot, with a small posse of her friends all around her. Mom turned and walked to the other side of the room, missing the smug expression on her adversary's face.

"Way to go. I love the energy, ladies," Marcel encouraged as Mom continued her gyrations. I would miss his enthusiasm, but I wasn't going to join this club.

The manager was waiting outside the door for us when class ended. I felt the stink eye from Chair Lady as she approached, opening her mouth to complain.

The manager said to Mom, "I was wondering if you would like to be Marcel's assistant? He needs support with the larger classes and tells me that you're just the person to help. He likes your can-do attitude. I've been watching, and I agree."

Mom beamed like she'd won a trophy. "That would be so much fun."

In that one moment, I knew two things. I would be back to walking our dog in peace, and Chair Lady would reclaim her coveted spot. Actually, three things. This year, Mom would be able to keep her resolution.

Visit Donna
At

www.donnatoddauthor.com

Amazon
https://goo.gl/CCpM4T